Scary Fairy Tales

The Snow Queen

and other stories

Compiled by Vic Parker

Miles Kelly

First published in 2012 by Miles Kelly Publishing Ltd
Harding's Barn, Bardfield End Green, Thaxted, Essex, CM6 3PX, UK

2 4 6 8 10 9 7 5 3 1

Publishing Director Belinda Gallagher
Creative Director Jo Cowan
Editor Sarah Parkin
Designer Jo Cowan
Editorial Assistants Lauren White, Amy Johnson
Production Manager Elizabeth Collins
Reprographics Stephan Davis, Jennifer Hunt, Thom Allaway

ISBN 978-1-84810-592-8

Printed in China

British Library Cataloguing-in-Publication Data
A catalogue record for this book is available from the British Library

ACKNOWLEDGEMENTS

The publishers would like to thank the following artists who have contributed to this book:

Cover: Cherie Zamazing at The Bright Agency
Advocate Art: Luke Finlayson
The Bright Agency: Peter Cottrill, Gerald Kelley, Cherie Zamazing

All other artwork from the Miles Kelly Artwork Bank

The publishers would like to thank the following source for the use of their photographs:
Shutterstock.com (cover) donatas1205, Eky Studio; (page decorations) alarik, dmiskv,
Ensuper, Eugene Ivanov, hugolacasse

Every effort has been made to acknowledge the source and copyright holder of each picture.
Miles Kelly Publishing apologises for any unintentional errors or omissions.

Made with paper from a sustainable forest

www.mileskelly.net   info@mileskelly.net

www.factsforprojects.com

CONTENTS

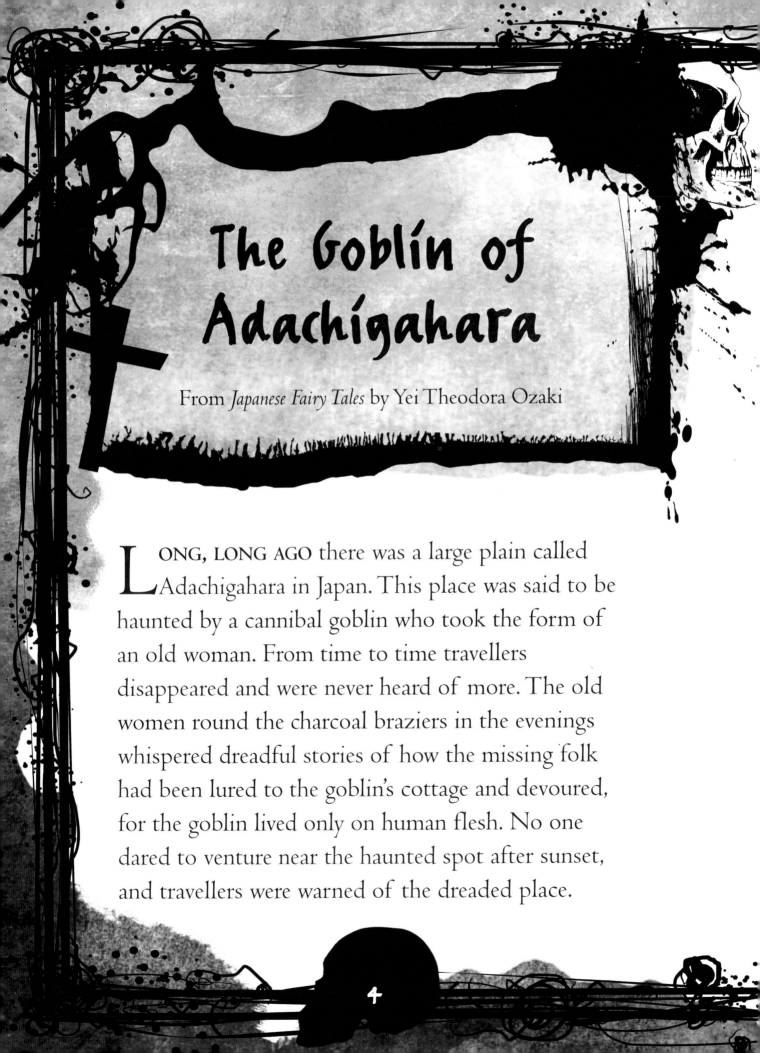

The Goblin of Adachigahara

From *Japanese Fairy Tales* by Yei Theodora Ozaki

LONG, LONG AGO there was a large plain called Adachigahara in Japan. This place was said to be haunted by a cannibal goblin who took the form of an old woman. From time to time travellers disappeared and were never heard of more. The old women round the charcoal braziers in the evenings whispered dreadful stories of how the missing folk had been lured to the goblin's cottage and devoured, for the goblin lived only on human flesh. No one dared to venture near the haunted spot after sunset, and travellers were warned of the dreaded place.

One day as the sun was setting, a priest came to the plain. His robe showed that he was a Buddhist pilgrim walking from shrine to shrine. He had apparently lost his way, and as it was late he met no one who could warn him of the haunted spot.

He had walked the whole day and was now very tired and hungry. The evenings were chilly, for it was late autumn, and he began to feel anxious to find a night's lodging. But he found himself lost in the midst of the large plain, and looked about in vain for some sign of human dwelling.

At last, after wandering about for some hours, he saw a clump of trees in the distance, and through the trees he caught sight of the glimmer of a ray of light.

Keeping the light before his eyes he dragged his weary, aching feet as quickly as he could towards the spot, and soon came to a miserable-looking little cottage. As he drew near he saw that it was in a tumble-down condition, the bamboo fence was broken and weeds and grass pushed their way through the gaps. The paper screens which serve as windows

and doors in Japan were full of holes, and the posts of the house seemed scarcely able to support the old thatched roof. The hut was open, and by the light of a lantern an old woman sat industriously spinning.

The pilgrim called to her and said: "Good evening, old woman – I am a traveller! Please excuse me, but I have lost my way and do not know what to do, for I have nowhere to rest tonight. I beg you to be good enough to let me spend the night under your roof."

The old woman, as soon as she heard herself spoken to, rose and approached the intruder.

"I am very sorry for you. You must indeed be distressed to have lost your way in such a spot so late at night. But unfortunately I cannot put you up, for I have no accommodation whatsoever for a guest in this poor lonely place!"

"Oh, that does not matter," said the priest, "all I want is a shelter under some roof for the night, and if you will be good enough just to let me lie on the floor I shall be grateful. I am too tired to walk further tonight, so I hope you will not refuse me." And in this way he pressed the woman to let him stay.

She seemed very reluctant, but at last she said: "Very well. I can offer you a poor welcome only, but come in and I will make a fire, for the night is cold."

The pilgrim was only too glad to do so. He took off his sandals and entered the hut. The old woman then lit the fire, and bade her guest draw near.

"You must be hungry after your long walk," said the old woman. "I will go and cook some supper for you." She then went to the kitchen to cook some rice.

After the priest had finished his supper the old

woman sat down by the fireplace, and they talked together for a long time. The pilgrim thought to himself that he had been very lucky to come across such a kind, hospitable old woman. At last the wood gave out, and as the fire died slowly down he began again to shiver with cold.

"I see you are cold," said the old woman; "I will go out and gather some more wood. You must stay here and take care of the house."

"No, no," said the pilgrim, "let me go instead, for you are old, and I cannot think of letting you go out to get wood for me on this cold night!"

The old woman shook her head and said: "You must stay quietly here, for you are my guest." Then she left him and went out.

In a minute she came back and said: "You must sit where you are, and whatever happens don't go near or look into the back room. Now mind what I tell you!"

The priest agreed, rather bewildered.

The old woman then went out again and the priest was left alone. The fire had died out and the only

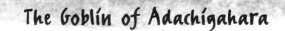

light in the hut was that of a dim lantern. For the first time that night he began to feel that he was in a weird place, and the old woman's words aroused his curiosity and his fear.

What hidden thing could be in that room that she did not wish him to see? For some time the remembrance of his promise kept him still, but at last he could no longer resist his curiosity to peep into the forbidden place.

He got up and began to move slowly towards the back room. Then the thought that the old woman would be very angry with him if he disobeyed her made him come back to his place by the fireside.

As the minutes went slowly by he began to feel more frightened, and to wonder what dreadful secret was in the room behind him. He must find out.

"She will not know that I have looked unless I tell her. I will just have a peep before she comes back."

With these words he got up on his feet and stealthily crept towards the forbidden spot. With trembling hands he pushed back the sliding door and looked in. What he saw froze the blood in his veins. The room was full of dead men's bones and the walls were splashed and the floor was covered with human blood. In one corner skull upon skull rose to the ceiling, in another was a heap of arm bones, in another a heap of leg bones. The sickening smell made him faint. He fell backwards with horror, and for some time lay in a heap on the floor. He trembled all over and his teeth chattered.

"How horrible!" he cried out. "What awful den have I come to on my travels? Is it possible that that kind old woman is really the cannibal goblin? When she comes back she will show herself and eat me up!"

With these words his strength came back to him and, snatching up his staff, he rushed out of the house. Out into the night he ran, his one thought to get as far as he could from the goblin's haunt. He had not gone very far when he heard steps behind him and a voice crying: "Stop! Stop, you wicked man!"

He ran on, doubling his speed. As he ran he heard the steps come nearer and nearer, and he recognised

the old woman's voice which grew louder and louder.

The priest quite forgot how tired he was and his feet flew over the ground faster than ever. Fear gave him strength, for he knew that if the goblin caught him he would soon be one of her victims. With all his heart he repeated the prayer to Buddha: "Namu Amida Butsu, Namu Amida Butsu."

And after him rushed the dreadful old hag, her face changing with rage into the demon that she was. In her hand she carried a large, bloodstained knife, and she still shrieked after him, "Stop! Stop!"

At last, when the priest felt he could run no more, the dawn broke, and with the darkness of night the goblin vanished. The priest now knew that he had met the Goblin of Adachigahara, the story of whom he had heard but never believed to be true. He felt that he owed his wonderful escape to the protection of Buddha, so he took out his rosary and, bowing his head as the sun rose, made his thanksgiving earnestly. He then set forward for another part of the country, glad to leave the haunted plain behind him.

The Snow Queen

An extract from the tale by Hans Christian Andersen

ONCE UPON A TIME there was a wicked sprite, who made a mirror which made all that was good and beautiful look poor and mean; while that which was good-for-nothing and ugly looked even more good-for-nothing and ugly. If a good thought passed through a man's mind, then a grin was seen in the mirror, and the sprite laughed heartily at his clever discovery. All the little sprites thought they would fly up to the sky and have a joke there. The higher they flew with the mirror, the more terribly it grinned: they could hardly hold it fast — suddenly the mirror shook so terribly with grinning, that it flew out of their hands and fell to the earth, where it was dashed in a hundred million and more pieces. And now it worked much more evil than before; for some of these pieces were hardly so large as a grain of sand, and they flew into people's eyes and then people were attracted to that which was evil. Some persons even got a splinter in their heart, and then their heart became like a lump of ice. Many of the splinters were carried aloft by the air, and then blown about the wide world.

At this time, there lived in a large town two little children – a boy called Kay and a girl named Gerda. They were not brother and sister; but they cared for each other as much as if they were. Their houses were next to each other – and there was to the roof of each house a small window. In summer, when the windows were open they could get to each other with one jump over the gutter. The children liked nothing more than to sit together at the windows and talk, holding each other by the hand, often kissing the

roses in their window boxes and looking up at the clear sunshine.

One day, Kay and Gerda were at the windows, looking at a picture book, when Kay said, "Oh! I feel such a sharp pain in my heart; and now something has got into my eye!"

The little girl put her arms around his neck. He winked his eyes; now there was nothing to be seen.

"I think it is out now," said he; but it was not. It was just one of those pieces of glass from the magic mirror that had got into his eye; and poor Kay had got another piece right in his heart.

"You look so ugly!" he suddenly said to Gerda. "And these roses are very ugly, just like the boxes they are planted in!" And then he gave a box a good kick with his foot, and pulled a rose up.

"What are you doing?" cried the little girl; and as he perceived her fright, he pulled up another rose, got in at the window, and hastened off.

Afterwards, he was able to imitate the gait and manner of everyone in the street. Everything that was peculiar and displeasing in them, Kay knew how to imitate, and make everybody laugh – except the person being made fun of! But it was the glass he had got in his eye; the glass that was sticking in his heart, which made him tease even little Gerda, whose whole soul was devoted to him.

One winter's day, when flakes of snow were flying about, he spread the skirts of his blue coat, and caught the snow as it fell.

"Look through this glass, Gerda," said he. And every flake seemed larger, and appeared like a magnificent flower, or a beautiful star; it was splendid to look at!

"Look, how clever!" said Kay. "That's much more interesting than real flowers!"

It was not long after this, that Kay came one day with large gloves on, and his little sledge at his back, and bawled into Gerda's ears, "I have permission to go out into the square where the others are playing;" and off he was in a moment.

There, in the market place, some of the boldest

boys used to tie their sledges to the carts as they passed by, and so they were pulled along, and got a good ride. Soon a large sledge passed by: it was painted quite white, and there was someone in it wrapped up in a rough white mantle of fur, with a rough white fur cap on his head. The sledge drove round the square twice, and Kay tied on his sledge as quickly as he could, and off he drove with it. On they went quicker and quicker into the next street; and the person who drove turned round to Kay and nodded to him in a friendly manner, just as if they knew each other. Every time he was going to untie his sledge, the person nodded to him, and then Kay sat quiet; and so on they went till they came outside the gates of the town. Then the snow began to fall so thickly that Kay could not see an arm's length before him, but still on he went. Suddenly he let go of the string he held in his hand in order to get loose from the sledge, but it was no use; still the little vehicle rushed on with the quickness of the wind. He then cried as loud as he could, but no one heard him; the snow drifted and the sledge flew on, and sometimes it gave a jerk as though they were driving over hedges and ditches. Kay was quite frightened, and he tried to repeat the Lord's Prayer; but he was only able to remember his times tables.

The snowflakes grew larger and larger, till at last they looked just like great white fowls. Suddenly they flew on one side; the large sledge stopped, and the person who drove rose up. It was a lady; her cloak and cap were of snow. She was tall and of slender figure, and of a dazzling whiteness. It was the Snow Queen.

"We have travelled fast," said she; "but it is freezing cold. Come under my bearskin." And she put him in the sledge beside her, wrapped the fur round him, and he felt as though he were sinking in a snow drift.

"Are you still cold?" asked she; and then she kissed his forehead. Ah! It was colder than ice; it penetrated to his very heart, which was already almost a frozen lump; it seemed to him as if he were about to die – but a moment more and it was quite congenial to him, and he did not notice the cold that was around him.

"My sledge! Do not forget my sledge!" It was the first thing he thought of. But it was there tied to one of the white chickens, who flew along with it on his back behind the large sledge. The Snow Queen kissed Kay once more, and then he forgot little Gerda, grandmother, and all whom he had left at his home.

Kay thought she was very beautiful; in his eyes she was perfect, and he did not fear her at all. He looked upwards in the large, huge empty space above him, and on she flew with him; flew high over the black clouds, while the storm moaned and whistled as though it were singing some old tune. On they flew over woods and lakes, over seas, and many lands; and beneath them the chilling storm rushed fast, the wolves howled, the snow crackled; above them flew large screaming crows, but higher up appeared the moon, quite large and bright; and it was on it that Kay gazed during the long, long winter's night; while by day he slept at the feet of the Snow Queen.

What became of little Gerda when Kay did not return? Where could he be? Nobody knew; nobody could give any information. All the boys knew was that they had seen him tie his sledge to another large, splendid one, which drove down the street and out of the town. Nobody knew where he was; many sad tears were shed, and little Gerda wept long and bitterly.

At last she said that he must have been drowned in the river which flowed close to the town – that alas, he must be dead!

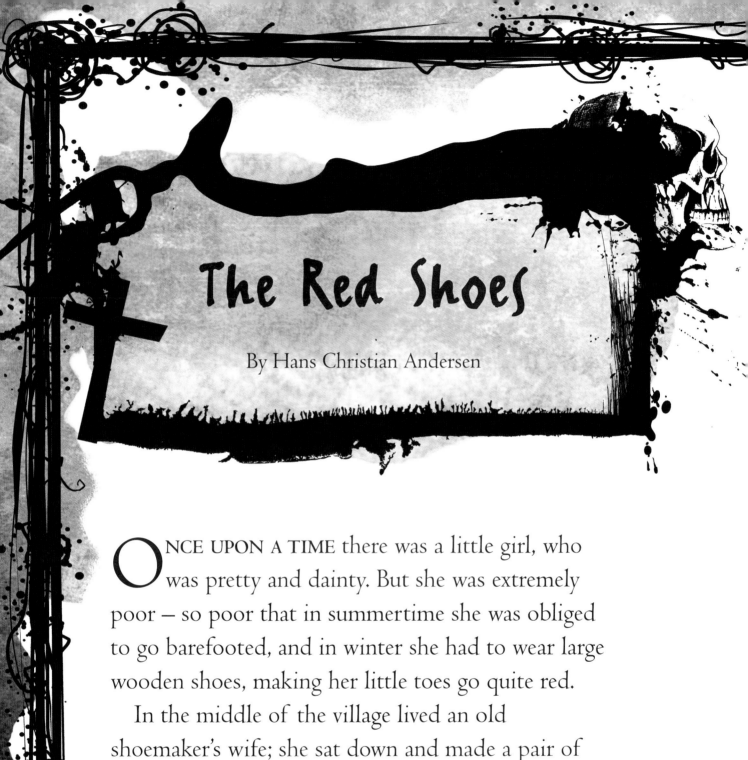

The Red Shoes

By Hans Christian Andersen

ONCE UPON A TIME there was a little girl, who was pretty and dainty. But she was extremely poor – so poor that in summertime she was obliged to go barefooted, and in winter she had to wear large wooden shoes, making her little toes go quite red.

In the middle of the village lived an old shoemaker's wife; she sat down and made a pair of little shoes out of some old pieces of red cloth. They were clumsy, but she meant well, for they were intended for the little girl, whose name was Karen.

Karen wore them for the first time on the day of

her mother's funeral. They were not suitable for mourning; but she had no others, so she put her bare feet into them and walked behind the humble coffin.

Just then a large carriage came by, and in it sat an old lady; she looked at the little girl, and taking pity on her, said to the clergyman, "Look here, if you will give me the little girl, I will take care of her."

Karen believed that this was all on account of the red shoes, but the old lady thought them hideous, so they were burned. Karen was dressed very neatly and cleanly; she was taught to read and to sew, and people said that she was pretty.

One day the queen was travelling through that part of the country and had her little daughter with her. All the people, amongst them Karen too, streamed towards the castle, where the little princess, in fine white clothes, stood before the window and allowed herself to be stared at. She wore neither a train nor a golden crown, but beautiful, red Morocco shoes.

Karen was now old enough to have a special ceremony at church called confirmation; for this

important occasion she received some new clothes and she was also to have new shoes. The rich shoemaker in the town took the measure of her little foot in his own room, in which there stood great glass cases full of pretty shoes and white slippers. It all looked lovely, but the old lady could not see very well. Amongst the shoes stood a pair of red ones, like those which the princess had worn. The shoemaker said that they had been made for a count's daughter, but that they had not fitted.

"I suppose they are of patent leather?" asked the old lady. "They shine so."

"Yes, they do," said Karen. They fitted her, and were bought. But the old lady knew nothing of them being red, for she would never have allowed Karen to be confirmed in bright, bold red shoes, as she was now to be.

The whole of the way from the church door to the choir it seemed to Karen as if even the ancient figures on the monuments, in their stiff collars and long black robes, had their

eyes fixed on her red shoes. It was only of these that she thought when the clergyman laid his hand upon her head and spoke of the holy baptism and told her that she was now to be a grown-up Christian.

In the afternoon the old lady heard from everybody that Karen had worn red shoes. She said that it was a shocking thing to do, and that Karen was always to go to church in future in black shoes, even if they were old.

On the following Sunday there was Communion at Mass. Karen looked first at the black shoes, then put on the red ones.

The sun was shining gloriously, so Karen and the old lady went along the footpath, where it was dusty. At the church door stood an old crippled soldier leaning on a crutch; he had a wonderfully long beard, more red than white, and he asked the old lady whether he might wipe her shoes. Then Karen put out her little foot too. "Dear me, what pretty dancing shoes!" said the soldier. "Sit fast, when you dance," said he, addressing the shoes. The old lady gave the soldier some money and then went into the church.

And all the people inside looked at Karen's red shoes, and all the figures gazed at them; when Karen knelt before the altar and put the golden goblet to her mouth, she thought only of the red shoes. It seemed as though they were swimming in the goblet, and she forgot to sing the hymns, and to say the Lord's Prayer.

Now everyone came out of church, and the old lady stepped into her carriage. But just as Karen was lifting up her foot to get in, the old soldier said: "Dear me, what pretty dancing shoes!" and Karen could not help it, she was obliged to dance a few steps; and once she had begun, her legs continued to dance. She could not stop; the coachman had to run after her and seize her. He lifted her into the carriage, but her feet continued to dance, so that she kicked the good old lady violently. At last they took off her shoes and her legs were at rest.

Now the old lady fell ill, and it was said that she would not rise from her bed again. She had to be nursed and waited upon,

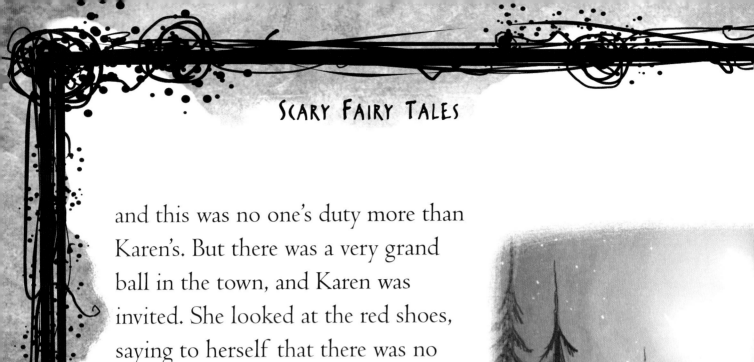

and this was no one's duty more than Karen's. But there was a very grand ball in the town, and Karen was invited. She looked at the red shoes, saying to herself that there was no sin in doing that; she put the red shoes on, thinking there was no harm in that either; and then she went to the ball; and commenced to dance.

But when she wanted to go to the right, the shoes danced to the left, and when she wanted to dance up the room, they danced down the room, down the stairs, through the street, and out through the town's gates. She danced, and was obliged to dance, far into the dark wood. Suddenly something shone up among the trees, and she believed it was the moon, for it was a face. But it was the old soldier with the red

beard; he sat there nodding and said: "Dear me, what pretty dancing shoes!"

She was frightened, and wanted to throw the shoes away; but they stuck fast. She tore off her stockings, but the shoes had grown fast to her feet. She danced and was obliged to go on dancing over field and meadow, in rain and sunshine, by night and by day – but by night it was most horrible.

She danced into the open churchyard; but the dead there did not dance. As she danced past the church door she saw an angel there in long white robes, with wings reaching down to the earth; his face was grave, and he held a broad, shining sword.

"Dance you shall," said he, "dance

in your red shoes till your skin shrivels up and you are a skeleton! Dance you shall, from door to door, and where proud and wicked children live you shall knock, so that they may hear you and fear you! Dance you shall, dance!"

"Mercy!" cried Karen. But the shoes carried her through the gate into the fields, along highways and byways, and unceasingly she had to dance.

One morning she danced past a door that she knew well; they were singing a hymn inside, and a coffin was being carried out. Then she knew that she was damned by the angel of God.

She danced, and was obliged to go on dancing through the dark night. The shoes bore her away over thorns and stumps till she was all torn and bleeding; she danced away over the heath to a lonely little house. Here, she knew, lived the executioner; and she tapped at the window and said: "Come out, come out! I cannot come in, for I must dance."

And the executioner said: "I don't suppose you know who I am. I strike off the heads of the wicked, and I notice that my axe is tingling to do so."

"Don't cut off my head," said Karen, "for then I could not repent; cut off my feet with the red shoes!" And then she confessed her sin, and the executioner struck off her feet with the red shoes; but the shoes danced away with the little feet into the deep forest.

Then he carved her a pair of wooden feet and some crutches, and taught her a hymn which is sung by sinners; she kissed the hand that guided the axe.

"Now, I have suffered enough for the red shoes," she said; "I will go to church, so that people can see me." And she went quickly up to the church door; but when she got there, the red shoes were dancing before her, and she was frightened, and turned back.

During the whole week she wept many bitter tears, but when Sunday came again she said: "Now I have suffered and striven enough." And so she went boldly on; but she had not got farther than the churchyard gate when she saw the red shoes dancing along before her. She became terrified, and turned back.

She went to the parsonage, and begged that she might be taken into service there. She would be industrious, she said, and do everything that she could; she did not mind about the wages as long as she had a roof over her and was with good people. The pastor's wife had pity on her, and took her in. And she was industrious and thoughtful. All the children liked her very much, but when they spoke about grandeur and beauty she would shake her head.

On the following Sunday they all went to church, and she was asked whether she wished to go too; but she looked sadly at her crutches. The others went to hear God's Word, but she went alone into her little room. Here she sat down with her hymn book, and as she was reading it, the wind carried the notes of the organ over to her from the church, and in tears she lifted her face and said: "O God, help me!"

Then the sun shone so brightly, and right before her stood an angel of God in white robes; it was the same one whom she had seen that night at the church door. He now carried a beautiful green branch, full of roses; with this he touched the ceiling, which rose up very high, and where he had touched it there shone a golden star. He touched the walls, which opened wide apart, and she saw the organ which was pealing forth; she saw the pictures of the old pastors and their wives, and the congregation sitting in the polished chairs singing from their hymn books. The church itself had come to the poor girl in her narrow room, or the room had gone to the church. She sat in the pew with the rest of the pastor's household, and when they had finished the hymn and looked up, they said, "It was right of you to come, Karen."

"It was mercy," said she.

The organ played and the children's voices in the choir sounded soft and lovely. The bright, warm sunshine streamed through the window into the pew where Karen sat, and her heart became so filled with joy, that it broke. Her soul flew on the sunbeams to heaven, and no one there asked after the red shoes.

The Rose Tree

From *English Fairy Tales* by Joseph Jacobs

THERE WAS ONCE a good man who had two children: a girl by a first wife, and a boy by the second. The girl was as white as milk and her lips were like cherries. Her hair was like golden silk and it hung to the ground. The girl's brother loved her dearly, but her wicked stepmother hated her.

"Child," said the stepmother one day, "go to the grocer's and buy me a pound of candles." She gave her the money; and the little girl went, bought the candles, and started on her return. There was a stile to cross. She put down the candles whilst she got over. Up came a dog and ran off with the candles.

She went back to the grocer's and she got a second bunch. She came to the stile, set down the candles, and proceeded to climb over. Up came the dog and ran off with the candles.

She went again to the grocer's and she got a third bunch; and just the same happened. Then she came to her stepmother crying, for she had spent all the money and had lost three bunches of candles.

The stepmother was angry, but she pretended not to mind the loss. She said to the child: "Come, lay your head on my lap that I may comb your hair." So the little one laid her head in the woman's lap, who proceeded to comb the yellow silken hair. And when she combed the hair fell over her knees and rolled right down to the ground.

Then the stepmother hated her more for the beauty of her hair; so she said to her, "I cannot part your hair on my knee, fetch me a block of wood." So the little girl fetched it. Then said the stepmother, "I cannot part your hair with a comb, fetch me an axe."

So the little girl fetched it.

"Now," said the wicked woman, "lay your head down on the block whilst I part your hair."

Well! She laid down her little golden head without fear; and whist! Down came the axe, and it was off. So the stepmother wiped the axe and laughed.

Then she took the heart and liver of the little girl, and she stewed them and brought them into the house for supper. The husband tasted them and

shook his head. He said they tasted very strangely.
She gave some to the little boy, but he would not eat
them. She tried to force him, but he refused, and ran
out into the garden, and took up his little sister, and
put her in a box, and buried the box under a rose tree;
and every day he went to the tree and wept, till his
tears ran down on the box.

One day the rose tree flowered. It was spring, and
there among the flowers was a white bird; and it sang,
and sang, and sang like an angel out of heaven. Away
it flew, and it went to a cobbler's shop, and perched
itself on a tree close by; and thus it sang,

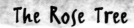

> "*My wicked mother slew me,*
>   *My dear father ate me,*
>   *My little brother whom I love*
>   *Sits below, and I sing above*
>   *Stick, stock, stone dead.*"

"Sing again that beautiful
song," asked the shoemaker.

"If you will first give me those little red shoes you
are making,"said the bird. The cobbler gave the shoes,

and the bird sang the song; then flew to a tree in front of a watchmaker's, and sang:

> "My wicked mother slew me,
>   My dear father ate me,
>   My little brother whom I love
>   Sits below, and I sing above
>   Stick, stock, stone dead."

"Oh, the beautiful song! Sing it again, sweet bird," asked the watchmaker.

"If you will give me first that gold watch and chain in your hand," said the bird. The jeweller gave the watch and chain. Then the bird took it in one foot, the shoes in the other, and, after having repeated the song, flew away to where three millers were picking a millstone. The bird perched on a tree and sang:

> "My wicked mother slew me,
>   My dear father ate me,
>   My little brother whom I love
>   Sits below, and I sing above
>   Stick!"

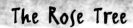

Then one of the men put down his tool and looked up from his work, "*Stock!*"

Then the second miller's man laid aside his tool and looked up, "*Stone!*"

Then the third miller's man laid down his tool and looked up, "*Dead!*"

Then all three cried out with one voice: "Oh, what a beautiful song! Sing it, sweet bird, again."

"If you will put the millstone round my neck," said the bird. The men did what the bird wanted and away to the tree it flew with the millstone round its neck, the red shoes in one foot, and the gold watch and chain in the other. It sang the song and then flew home. It rattled the millstone against the eaves of the house, and the stepmother said: "It thunders." Then the little boy ran out to see the thunder, and down dropped the red shoes at his feet. The bird rattled the millstone against the eaves of the house once more, and the stepmother said again: "It thunders." Then the father ran out and down fell the watch and chain about his neck.

In ran the father and son, laughing and saying,
"See, what fine things the thunder has brought us!"
Then the bird rattled the millstone
against the eaves of the house a third time;
and the stepmother said: "It thunders,
perhaps the thunder has brought something
for me," and she ran out; but the moment
she stepped outside the door, down fell
the millstone on her head; and so
she died.